LOST KITTIES

SQUAD GOALS
#ADORBS

written by
Maggie Fischer

fun
studio
INTERNATIONAL

P1 **PRE-LEVEL 1: ASPIRING READERS**

1 **LEVEL 1: EARLY READERS**

2 **LEVEL 2: DEVELOPING READERS**

3 **LEVEL 3: ENGAGED READERS**

- Repetition of longer sentence patterns with variation of placement of subjects, verbs, and adjectives
- Most of the vocabulary should be familiar to first graders
- Introduction of more complex spelling patterns and letter-sound relationships

4 **LEVEL 4: FLUENT READERS**

Studio Fun International
An imprint of Printers Row Publishing Group
A division of Readerlink Distribution Services, LLC
10350 Barnes Canyon Road, Suite 100, San Diego, CA 92121
www.studiofun.com

Written by Maggie Fischer
Illustrated by Hasbro and Tina Francisco &
Michael Bartolo of Glass House Graphics
Designed by Kara Kenna

HASBRO and its logo, LOST KITTIES and all related characters
are trademarks of Hasbro and are used with permission.
© 2019 HASBRO.

Printers Row Publishing Group is a division of Readerlink Distribution Services, LLC.
Studio Fun International is a registered trademark of Readerlink Distribution Services, LLC.
All notations of errors or omissions should be addressed to Studio Fun International,
Editorial Department, at the above address.

ISBN: 978-0-7944-4418-1

Manufactured, printed, and assembled in Shenzhen, China. First printing, January 2019. RRD/01/19

23 22 21 20 19 1 2 3 4 5

Licensed by:

TABLE of CONTENTS

NAP-KIN'S NOISY DAY   4

BONBON'S BAKING BLUNDER   10

PIXIE PURRS'S PEACEFUL POSE   16

TICKLES TV   22

MEMEZ'S MASTER MOVES   28

NAP-KIN'S NOISY DAY

NAP-KIN HAS REACHED THE IDEAL LEVEL OF COZINESS.

He's just starting to drift off, hoping to pilot his dream spaceship, when it happens—**CLANK**! **CRUNCH**! **WHIRR**!

Nap-kin's eyes fly open. Who is making this kind of racket at two in the afternoon? Don't they know that some kitties are still in bed?

Peeking out the window, Nap-kin sees the garbage truck **CREAKING** down the street. Nap-kin groans. He won't get any sleep until the truck leaves.

What seems like hours later, the garbage truck pulls away from Nap-kin's neighborhood. But the poor kitty is too wired to sleep now!

"Tomorrow, I'll try again," Nap-kin declares.

The next afternoon, Nap-kin decides to snooze in the basement. No garbage trucks to hear down there! Tossing his blankets onto a beanbag chair, Nap-kin flops down and starts to snooze.

Nap-kin is flying his dream spaceship through the galaxy. He passes planets that look like fish.

Suddenly, his spaceship starts to **BEEP** and **SHAKE**. Noises and bright lights get louder and louder until . . . Nap-kin wakes up with a shout!

Blinking, Nap-kin looks around the basement.
Eugene and Flakes are playing their electric guitars.
A disco ball is spinning, and the **THUMPING** music
is giving Nap-kin a whisker ache.

"HEY!" Nap-kin shouts. "I'm trying to sleep!"

"Aw, come on, Nap-kin," Eugene protests. "Can't
you nap somewhere else?"

Nap-kin sighs, and trudges upstairs.

Nap-kin is starting to worry. He still hasn't found the perfect napping place! Exhausted, he stumbles into the first door he sees.

"**CANNONBAAAAALL**!"

A giant splash hits Nap-kin in the face, and he blinks, sputtering. Nap-kin groans—he's in the bathroom! Flush waves at him as she dives in and out of the toilet. Nap-kin wrings the water from his fur and leaves in a rush.

Fed up, Nap-kin finally just curls up onto the floor. He's almost asleep when he hears it: **BEAUTIFUL** music!

Opening his eyes, Nap-kin sees Meowzart playing the keyboard with her eyes closed. Suddenly, her eyes snap open.

"Sorry, Nap-kin. Were you trying to sleep? I can play somewhere else!" the musical kitty says.

"No, no, it's wonderful! Keep playing. I'm just going to—" Nap-kin breaks off mid-sentence as he starts to **SNORE**. Meowzart giggles.

Sweet dreamz, Nap-kin!

2 BONBON'S BAKING BLUNDER

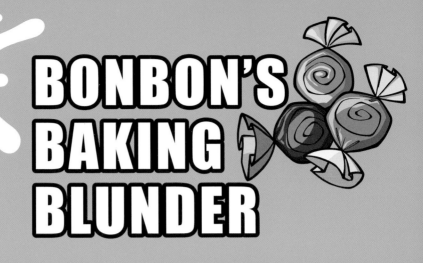

BONBON LEAPS UP FROM HER SEAT WHEN SHE HEARS THE OVEN TIMER.

Her cookies are ready! Excited, Bonbon puts on her oven mitts and pulls the tray out of the oven. The smell of catnip fills the kitchen. Closing her eyes, Bonbon takes a bite of one of the cookies—**PURR-FECT**!

A groan suddenly breaks the silence. Tummy Tum stands there, looking pained.

"What's wrong?" Bonbon asks.

"I'm SO hungry! This is the end! I can't go on!" Tummy Tum replies.

Bonbon laughs, handing her friend the freshly baked cookies. Tummy Tum grins, licking her lips. Bonbon turns to clean up when she hears a noisy gulp. Bonbon looks over and gasps: every single cookie is GONE!

"What happened to the cookies?" Bonbon asks Tummy Tum, shocked.

I atez them all. OOPZ!

Bonbon can't believe Tummy Tum's tiny tummy can fit so much food!

"I'm still so hungry, Bonbon!" Tummy Tum whines. Bonbon decides to make a **GIANT** batch of brownies! She gets to work in the kitchen, mixing brownie batter.

Finally, Bonbon slides a pan of brownie batter into the oven.

The timer dings and Bonbon takes the brownies out. She slides them over to Tummy Tum, who **ATTACKS** the new tray of treats. This time, Bonbon watches as Tummy Tum demolishes the brownies.

Tummy Tum looks at Bonbon expectantly and rubs her stomach. Bonbon sighs.

"Let me look at my recipes," she tells Tummy Tum.

Bonbon hunts through her recipes until she spots a hand-written note. Ah-ha! It's Great-Grandkitty Bonbon's taffy recipe! Stretchy taffy is the perfect treat to fill Tummy Tum!

Bonbon starts to boil sugar and butter, pouring food coloring in to make it a bright pink. Then she starts to **STRETCH** the mixture, pulling until the pink taffy fills her kitchen!

Bonbon heaves a giant armful of taffy onto a plate in front of Tummy Tum.

"Eat," Bonbon says, panting. Tummy Tum starts to gobble! The candy sticks to her stomach, making her FULL for the first time in . . . well, ever! After nearly *six* hours of eating, Tummy Tum leans back, letting out a breath.

Bonbon smiles, holding out another plate of taffy.

"Still hungry?" Bonbon asks sweetly.

There iz no roomy room in this TUMMY TUM!

3 PIXIE PURRS'S PEACEFUL POSE

PIXIE PURRS IS LOOKING FOR HER NEXT SNOOZING SPOT.

Cat bed? Boring. Cat tree? Next! Couch?

No thanks. But wait—what's that over there?

A black rectangle lies on the coffee table.

Francis' laptop: **PURR-FECT**!

Pixie Purrs lays down and purrs—nothing like a warm laptop to make your fur feel nice and toasty!

Closing her eyes, Pixie Purrs slowly drifts off to sleep. She dreams that schools of fish are swimming around the living room.

Sticking her tongue out with effort, Pixie Purrs stands on her tippy paws, trying to capture a fish as it floats by, and—**WHAM**!

She falls off of the coffee table and onto the floor. The impact wakes her, and she groans.

"What happened?" she mumbles.

No cat hair on my work laptop, Pixie! I haz told u that!

"Oh, Francis, take the burr out of your fur!" Pixie Purrs says. "Haven't you ever had a napping spot that was just too comfy to pass up?"

"I don't have *time* for naps," Francis frowns. He turns to leave the room, but he trips and steps on his tail. He stops suddenly, letting out a **YOWL**.

Pixie Purrs gasps when she sees his tail bent at an angle. That has to hurt! "Francis, I know how to help! You need to stretch. Let's do yoga!" Pixie Purrs says excitedly.

"I don't have time to waste on pointless posing," Francis snaps.

"Oh come on, Francis!" Pixie Purrs says, grabbing Francis by the paw. The two kitties stop at Pixie Purrs's meditation spot. Fluffy pillows cover the floor, and tinkly wind chimes sound from the window.

"Now, sit here," Pixie Purrs demands, pointing to one of the pillows. Grumbling, Francis takes a seat.

"Breathe in. Now, out. Keep going," Pixie Purrs coaches. The two kitties stretch through Downward-Facing Cat pose, followed by Kitten's pose, and ending with Cat Tree pose. Finally, they end up lying flat on their mats, breathing deeply.

Pixie Purrs pops up to ask Francis how he's feeling, but the grumpy kitty is fast **ASLEEP**! His tail is back to normal. Francis snores, and Pixie Purrs chuckles. Now, where did Francis put his laptop? It's time for the rest of her nap . . .

4 TICKLES TV

IT'S A BEAUTIFUL SUNNY DAY, AND TICKLES IS IN THE MOOD TO GO OUTSIDE!

On his way out, Tickles passes the living room. Chickie is on the couch, flipping through TV channels.

"Wow, you're changing channels so fast!" Tickles says. But Tickles sometimes trips over his *L*s and *R*s, so it sounds more like: "Wow, yoh changing channohs so fast!"

Tickles leaves Chickie to his channel surfing, and heads to the garden. His favorite thing to do outside is to visit all of his butterfly friends!

Little does Tickles know that prankster Pants has a trick up his sleeve today. When Tickles was getting ready in the morning, Pants put sugar in Tickles's soap. There's nothing that butterflies love more than sugar water, and now Tickles is a walking **SWEET TREAT**!

Pants sneaks behind his friend as he walks through the garden, waiting for him to get butterfly **TICKLED**! But Tickles is having fun, laughing as butterflies land on his fur and give him butterfly kisses. Pants shrugs. It's hard to prank Tickles—he's happy no matter what!

"I bet if Chickie saw these magic butterflies, he'd find it as fun as I do," Tickles thinks to himself. "I'll put on a butterfly show! Now *that* is something Chickie hasn't seen before!"

Tickles gets to work, putting together a costume. He dresses up as a big kitty butterfly to lead the other butterflies around.

Finally, the show is ready! The last thing left to do is get the butterflies inside the house. It shouldn't be a problem for Tickles and his magic touch. But the butterflies are just flying around aimlessly!

"Come on, butterflies! It's time for the show!" Tickles tells them, worried. Suddenly, Pants runs up with a squirt bottle of soap.

HERE, TICKLES!

"It's my fault the butterflies were all over you this morning," Pants explains, "I put sugar in your soap as a prank. I'm sorry you're not really magic."

"That's okay!" Tickles says. "It sure *feels* like magic!" The kitties head into the living room and block the television.

"Huh?" Chickie says, surprised.

"Attention, kitties! Iz I! Dah biggest buttahfwy in the gawden!

Tickles starts to **DANCE** and **WIGGLE**! The cloud of butterflies follows, landing on him and flapping their wings. The kitties can't help but laugh!

"You're right, Tickles! I've never seen *that* before!" Chickie says, cracking up.

5 MEMEZ'S MASTER MOVES

MEMEZ IS PRACTICING FOR A SINGING CONTEST ON SATURDAY.

Memez can't resist a **SPOTLIGHT**. Finishing the final note of his song, Memez strikes a pose. He beams as the other kitties applaud.

"Bravo, bravo!" Chomp cheers, though it's hard to tell exactly what she's saying—her mouth is full of tacos.

Memez has the singing contest in the bag! As he gets up to leave, he sees that two kitties are still in the audience. Pepp and J. Roly sit, staring at Memez.

"Uh, hey there!" Memez says to his friends.

"Did you like the show?"

"Like it? Loved it! Best! Ever!" Pepp shouts, leaping with each word and striking a pose midair.

"But," J. Roly starts, and Pepp cuts in: "Your moves have no **POW**! No **BAM**! No **PEPP**!"

"My moves?" Memez asks.

"Your dance moves!" Pepp replies. "And no one can dance like J. Roly and me. Let's go!"

Pepp flies out of the door with J. Roly behind her. Memez follows the two kitties. A stereo is set up in the grass. J. Roly turns it on.

J. Roly starts to dance, moving and grooving with catlike grace! He even **FLIPS** onto the jelly jar on his head and spins!

Pepp joins in, starting to shimmy. She bounces up and down, backflipping into a kitty split! Shutting off the music, the two kitties look at Memez, grinning.

"Now it's your turn," Pepp says. "Follow our lead, and remember: the best dance moves are the ones that make you feel like yourself."

Nervous, Memez follows along as the kitties teach him step after step.

The day of the singing contest has arrived! Memez is worried about messing up. But he remembers what Pepp said: "the best dance moves are the ones that make you feel like **YOURSELF**."

When it's his turn, Memez owns the stage! As the last note plays, Memez slides into a final pose, smiling at the audience.

"Thanks for teaching me," Memez says to his friends as he leaves the stage. "I had so much fun!"